T0195081

Faith Based
Short Stories

Anna Hartsell

authorHOUSE®

AuthorHouse™
1663 Liberty Drive
Bloomington, IN 47403
www.authorhouse.com
Phone: 833-262-8899

Published by AuthorHouse 01/12/2022

ISBN: 978-1-6655-4748-2 (sc)
ISBN: 978-1-6655-4747-5 (e)

Library of Congress Control Number: 2021925453

Print information available on the last page.

Annie Can!

They said she couldn't, wouldn't

And she did!

Did what? You ask;

Well, she beat Cancer.

Not just any cancer,

But, stage 4 CML

And she accomplished this at just 1yr.

Can you do that?

Not many can, but

Annie Can!

She went to school and endured bullies because treatments like chemo and radiation made her shorter than others. She wore glasses too. Kids made fun and asked lots of questions. But Annie answered the best she could and coped by building walls to conceal her differences, and block people out, and keep people from knowing her. Annie wilted like a sun beaten flower. Her beautiful bright eyes and smiling face turned downward in hopes to avoid all people. She frowned, always consumed with worry. Mostly she worried about what others might think of her or worse, what they might say or do in reaction to her ability to stand out in a crowd. Annie kept everything inside like her feelings. She never told anyone.

Hiding the best she could in an all-seeing world, Annie went to college. She worked hard. Her final classes came around, but Annie broke into pieces. It was too much. She had a break in her mental health and was very sick for years to come. She did not even go to her college graduation.

After many tries, Dr. Green and Holly, my counselor, found the right medicine and Holly helped alleviate troubles that had been pinned inside for no one to see. Annie finally opened up about all that had ever bothered her and was able to let it go, once and for all.

Annie has always possessed a giving nature. She searched her heart and asked God for help in showing her what could be done with this broken mess. The answer came through experiences. Annie felt the excessive need to share her story with others who might be struggling. So she set out to do just that.

And from then on, she was able to give of herself, helping others in the process. Annie was a blooming flower again. Just as she started.

BECAUSE ANNIE CAN

YOU CAN TOO!

Meet Me at the Mailbox

By: Anna Hartsell

I was the tiniest in my class at school. I remember Mrs. Butler would pick me up so I could see what they were having for lunch in the cafeteria. I got knocked around at recess too. I was forever coming home with skint knees. Once my Dad asked me what my favorite part of the day was. I replied "Lunch and going home." He belly laughed and the statement remained true throughout my career as a student. The morning routine at our house was up to my Mom. Stories remain legendary! We would arrive in the car rider line at 8:06 a.m. to which my Mother would reply "People run a mile in four minutes, Run you can make it!" My bookbag which weighed as much or more than me would bounce back and forth on my back side the whole way. When I was nine, we moved to a different school. Making friends was never a strong suite. You may say I'm crazy but, I swear I knew about mean girls way before the movie. Animals became my new friends. We had 4 dogs at one time. My neighbor asked if we would take a stray. With some begging, my Mom agreed. I took the dog inside to hide from my Dad as he was coming home from work. We hid behind the door, but she slipped from my hold and scurried across the kitchen floor. He saw the flash of brown and black and knew we had something up our sleeves. I named her Little Bit. We had her for a couple years and we bought a golden retriever and named her Maggie. Fast forward a few more years and My Aunt Beth asked us to keep their golden retriever, Belvedere. We inherited him, that gets us to 3. And Little Bit had puppies! Rosie and Gus were their names. We gave Gus away, with lots of tears, and there you have my four best friends. Five if you include Max, Rosie's and Gus' father. Who belonged next door. So, I had a whole crew of furry friends just waiting for me when I got off the crazy school bus! They would meet me at the mailbox off a long gravel drive at the end of the cul de sac. It was the best years of my life. To make a rotten school day just wash away was no easy task, but together they did it with ease, bringing a smile to my face every time! Little Bit, Maggie, Belvedere, Rosie, and sometimes Max, have long since passed. But they served their purpose of making their owner, a downhearted little girl, laugh and smile and beam with pride as the four and sometimes five furry friends would meet her at the mailbox every weekday afternoon! If I couldn't find a friend at school, I knew I had a whole bunch waiting for me at home! Their story will remain legend as I pass this on to you. There is always someone to turn to to make you smile if you are having a hard time. Even if found in the dog kingdom! Animals understand more than we think and they know us better than we know ourselves sometimes! Just get whatever is bothering you off of your mind, it doesn't matter who is listening, human or canine. Just talk it out. You'd be surprised at the wonders it does of lifting the burden right off your shoulders. If your furry friends need a walk that is a great way to blow off steam as well. Remember to treat others with kindness and compassion. That always helps. Treat them as you want to be treated like the Bible says in Matthew 7:12. You have no idea what any one person is dealing with on the inside. One of my favorite quotes is this: "Just because someone carries it well doesn't mean it's not heavy." -unknown

You also can remind yourself to think good thoughts. After all those thoughts are what inspires action. The Bible speaks on this in Philippians 4:8. If your thoughts are good then your actions will be good. That will help not just you, but everyone you come in contact with. The point is not just keeping out of trouble at home and school, but to act in ways that show the world Jesus' love through you. He lives in your heart and wants only good for your life. Jeremiah 29:11. So think about these lessons I have learned the hard way. And learn from my mistakes!

You can do this because everyone who has Jesus in their heart can do all things through Christ who strengthens them. Philippians 4:13. I encourage you to do good in the world, and so will I.

For our present troubles are small and won't last very long. Yet they produce for us a glory that vastly outweighs them and will last forever. So we don't look at the troubles we can see now; rather we fix our gaze on things that cannot be seen. For the things we see now will soon be gone, but the things we cannot see will last forever. 2 Corinthians 4:17-18

New Living Translation

Be Silly.

Be Honest.

Be Kind.

-Ralph Waldo Emerson

The End.

Nobody Knows

An iconic line given by brilliant writers to Jerry Van Dyke as a guest star on his brother's hit show The Dick Van Dyke Show in the early nineteen sixties. True it was given the love sick character of Stacey. But I find it relevant to many other problematic situations in life. I find it helps relieve anger, stress, frustration, sadness, and complete loss of the thought process in general speaking of said mounding feelings! Go on, try it! The next time you find yourself in an argument, just shout "NOBODY KNOWS HOW I FEEL!" And nobody can take that away from you!

Why is a thirty something quoting a comedy series nearly sixty years to date? Because; she is forever an old soul, finding refuge in the genius of such comedic timing of souls that once wandered the world long before her own existence. Now, to be fair, I, the thirty something, have no concept of the business, I just find the quote memorable, hysterical, and useful! For many reasons.

The social discrepancies of childhood bullying are supposed to end at school, not follow you relentlessly through adulthood. Everyone grows up and moves on. But what if you don't. Everyone grows older, we are not talking Tuck Everlasting here. But I mean what if you don't necessarily grow *Up?*

I am 4 feet 5inches short and at no time am I going anywhere in the upward direction by any means of my own. Heels, ladies, are only made so tall. This does not seem a major feat, but let me tell you there are more people obligated to find the age old question of *Why t*han there are explanations! I have been questioned to no end regarding that very fact about myself.

It's true Nobody will ever know how it makes you feel unless you tell them. I have spent my life being quiet and reserved although at times, shocked, and never have I ever told one stranger how their rude comments make me feel. All through school my parents encouraged me to pray for my enemies and turn a blind eye, not because they didn't need to be called on it, but because I at no time owed them an explanation. I still maintain this stance. But I am tired of the criticism that befalls those who stray from the norm. Whatever that may be and whosoever came up with the standards! Who among us is normal enough to make such guidelines? No one is! People continue to state the obvious and speak the said difference as though they were the first and only to discover any difference at all. If you find yourself in my boat, please continue on.

Rather than lamenting, I aim to shed hope on the subject. I am not going to relive every account in which I was wronged, but give advice to you and me both. I will tell you this much. There is a night and day absolute change in the way I carried myself from birth and the time at which I entered Kindergarten. This is a major day because it forever changed me. I walk in and the fellow students want very much to know why I am so small. I told them I had Leukemia. They look at me with an upturned nose and say what's that? I then look to the teacher at which point she rescues me. Saying *cancer*. This is where fellow students want to know if they can catch it from me. I smile, thinking the whole exchange is odd. And politely say no. After I pass the inspection, I am led to be an accepted member of the class.

You might say kids are kids or they didn't know any better. What of the adults who continue to bully? But after that and to this day I feel I want to shout at them, something along the lines of Stacey's character, but would never do such a thing. These people never knew how it made me feel. So the blame falls on me, because I never told them. My advice to you and me is this. If you know of any moment in your life that specifically changed how you carry yourself, ***Live Each Day as If it Occured Before Said Turning Point. Live your days in joy and forget these people because I guarantee you they are*** *not, nor have they been replaying their exchange with you. Live as though you did before they told you you were wrong. That's it.* Think before you speak, my enemies, and I am praying for you! Please share if you found this at all helpful!

From Where I Stand

From where I stand, my view is modified according to height. I don't suppose I'd see much past your right elbow! Literally, I stand about a foot shorter than the average woman. We'll just let that sink in for a minute. My stance on life is likely nothing you've heard before. I have never expressed hurt feelings in real time. I have a million and one comebacks never to be verbalized. The afflicted encounter runs through my mind like a blooper reel. Anyone know what it's like being immeasurable to the world's standards? Well, I have a heap of life experience on that! Just wait! I will never: Have what you have. Do what you do. Look like you look. Think like you think. Throughout my childhood, all I wanted was to be invisible. To blend in. It has taken a lifetime to realize that' s never going to happen. I am original. As is each person ever created by God. I will tell you I have a choice to be consumed by the majority, or I can embrace my flaws, which do not exist according to God, God says we are made in His image. The man who knew no sin. He wants to save us from ourselves. If only we'd let Him. If we can just wrap our heads around this concept, each soul would benefit. If you find yourself on the outside looking in, join me as we make small steps into the crowd penetrating them with Christlike love. First we need our armor. Do you know what a child of God's armor looks like? It's not heavy or cumbersome at all. I will wear my armor and you can too and together we will make the world a better place. One encounter at a time. Ephesians 6:13 instructs us so. Therefore, put on every piece of God's armor so you will be able to resist the enemy in the time of evil. Then after the battle you will still be standing firm. Stand your ground, putting on the belt of truth and the body armor of God's righteousness. For shoes, put on the peace that comes from the Good News so that you will be fully prepared. In addition to all of these, hold up the shield of faith to stop the fiery arrows of the devil.

Put on salvation as your helmet, and take the sword of the Spirit, which is the word of God. Do you know what the Good News is? It's this: God loved us so much that he gave his only son to save us. John 3:16. There. Now you have everything you need to battle the worldly standards of today and greet each one that claims you don't belong with a loving heart. The Bible says this is like heaping burning coals on his head. Romans 12:20 Just tell them you knew that. The world is a temporary home. We, who stand with Christ belong to his home which is heaven. Through Him, we are granted eternal life with no more sorrow, heartache, sin or brokenness. If you come across someone who you cannot encourage, the Bible says to shake the dust from that place off your feet and move on. Let it go and keep on encouraging. Matthew 10:14.

Words

FAITH BASED SHORT STORIES

Words are spoken to us, for us, against us, over us, or about us. We cannot control how others perceive. But we have the power within to delegate the lifetime of said words. They can live in a memory or text for years and our brains keep returning to that word. To relive it even if it is bad, the bad just seems to confirm our deepest, darkest convictions when we are down. You are in control, however, of how often you let those words live in your mind and how often you revisit the encounter whether good or bad. Don't torment yourself. Re-visit the good and throw out the bad. It has no value to you.

Words used to shut me down. Harsh words would just make me crumble and be defeated. I had knock down, drag out fights with my mother and sister that drove my father out of the house for the duration of the weapon slinging. No punches were thrown, no physical interaction was engaged. But we knew enough to be lethal with our words. You have a choice also, whether you are going to speak life into someone or deliver a deadly blow with each breath you exhale. That's quite some power you are holding!

I have been the one slinging deadly blows and receiving them. Both shoes have been worn in one day. Because we are human. The best we can do is try to emulate Jesus' way and teachings to our fellow man. And ask for forgiveness the rest of the time. We live for a merciful God who understands the very fall of humankind from the beginning of Adam and Eve. There is nothing our God can't handle. Nothing too big, or scary or wrong or unbelievable that he cannot handle. And you know what? Nothing can separate our hearts from him. *Nothing. Romans 8:38 says this: And I am convinced that nothing can ever separate us from God's love. Neither death nor life, neither angels nor demons, neither our fears for today nor our worries for tomorrow- not even the powers of hell can separate us from God's love. He loves us unconditionally and nothing can erase that love.*

Be a bearer of light. Make it your goal to brighten someone's day especially if no one has brightened yours. You will benefit from great joy that exudes such encounters. Good always prevails whether we see it or not. *God works everything out for the good of those who love God. Romans 8:28.* You have nothing to lose. Stop holding to the shreds of what we think is good and look out for what is best to knock us off our feet! It's here. Right around the corner! We just have to tread lightly to find ourselves consumed by God's goodness!

Circumstances

how you deal with people and

darken a perfectly good and caring

bitter or angry. Those emotions have

a place. Just breathe! Take it in and know

meone who took on the world and its sin in the

gest sacrifice ever made by man, knows you and your

situation! He knows our days are numbered, but loves us

more and wants to bring us home more than anybody

can convey. Take heart, for I have overcome the world!

John 16:33 NLT I feel a gracious plenty safe and calm,

reassured, and loved, knowing a man named Jesus has

got this figured out....because I am lost, completely and

utterly lost. Anxious, nervous, afraid, overwhelmed about

an uncertain future Etc, Etc. Etc. Waiting news of "Is

this cancer?" "How bad is it?" I will know and understand

more in the days to come, and not until.

From here to the
Cotton Patch

Genesis 2:7 Then the Lord God formed the man from the dust of the ground. He breathed the breath of life into the man's nostrils, and he became a living person.

Our lives are like sandcastles; built up for what seems a lifetime, and washed away by the evening waves. But do not fret. God says what we consider a lifetime is only a fraction of the life of eternity with God. For that is what we live for...knowing there is no end. That we will be healed with no ailments free to run and frolic and meet with long passed family. The other positive is that we will all be family in Christ, in harmony.

I have to think of heaven as my destination and home. I have been sick in increments that fall in decades. The Lord could have taken me oh I don't know how many times. So what I make of it is that I am still meant to be alive and fighting for that silly thing called quality of life!

I'm sure you've heard of the phrase "Live Like You Were Dying," made famous by Tim Mcgraw's hit song.

Live like you were leaving a legacy. Don't do anything you are not proud of or would not support otherwise. Think before you act, and be kind, always.

Seriously, I wish for you and me to live with no regrets. Do only what you intended and nothing else. No excuses. But, remember Jesus died for your sins. So, like I heard a pastor say once, you are forgiven of your past, present, and future. All you have to do is ask every day for God to forgive you when you slip up. It never meant, contrary to my original beliefs, that you have to keep a perfect record of points or a score, measuring against yourself. And wondering if you will be admitted into heaven. It doesn't mean you are free to sin all the more, but, instead, it means you are free from that worry. Made possible by a benevolent and loving God who calls you his son and daughter.

Somethings Don't Come Easy

As of June 3 2021, I have been sick. The days are getting longer and that's if I can remember what day of the week it is! They all seem to run together. Wake up, take medicine, eat protein packed food and sleep. Well, my mother and I are reading Because of Winn Dixie. My mom is an elementary school teacher and this Children's book is packed with wisdom.

I don't mind, you see I've been through it all before. Probably worse. I just don't remember enough to compare. IVs, pic lines, three surgeries, staples nothing but ice chips for a couple days and watching my Mom and Dad eat without their hands pinned to all those contraptions while mine were! It was a nightmare.

It wasn't all that bad, those were just bad days. I was in the hospital for thirty days. Yikes! People sent so much love and prayers and cards. My room was constantly full of flowers and an abundance of cards and well wishes. My sister, Taylor came and washed my oily bed head with a dry shampoo, a shower cap and a small bucket of water. This is all while I was half sitting in the hospital bed. How she managed all that is beyond me! She could have been shocked by all the wires behind there or I could have been very wet!

Everyone knows Jillian Michaels from the biggest loser. Well one of the first things my sister said to me was, "You'll be back on your Jillian workouts before you know it." I said in my best sarcastic, ho hum reply, "Not today."

Then we were discharged from the hospital, it was evening by the time we got home. I went up the back steps of the deck like usual and first thing I know I'm lying on the deck with a skint knee and very sore wounds elsewhere. Then I was being picked up by my parents like a puppy and here we go again.

Stubborn. That's what I am, because it has happened that way since. Again, I go for the steps and again I fall in the fetal position, letting out a yelp. Turns out I scraped the same knee as before and it hurt all the more! I told my Dad that I was sorry I had pulled the same ol' trick on him like an old mule! He gets after me for not waiting on someone to help me up the stairs! It's for my own good!

Practice and determination is what you need
to recover and will power to want to do better.
Funny, I never had any of those qualities when
I was taking piano lessons in grade school!

Final Words

My friend, and fellow reader, our time has come to a close. I just want to share a few more words of advice before I go. It has been a blast to enlighten you with stories from my childhood and adolescence of what I learned no matter how hard a lesson it seemed at the time. Let me say Thank you from the bottom of my heart for picking up this small book. It means the world to me! I have known two things in my life from a young age. One I have always wanted to write a book no matter how short! And two, I have it embedded in my heart to make a difference in someones' life for the better. I believe I can do those things because I have been writing to you, Yes! You! I sincerely hope you will take care of yourself and enjoy life to the fullest!

That short note being said, I have one more story to share with you. Do you ever worry constantly about every little thing especially in social situations? Well I can tell you it will not help it will only make you miserable! I know because I was like this for years until I received professional help and medicine to ease my troubles. It made a world of difference for me. I'm not trying to promote medicine or professional help, but sometimes help comes from where you would least seek it!

I have a personal all time favorite verse in the Bible. It is Matthew 6:25-34 NIV. Now it is quite longer than any other verse I have mentioned thus far. But just hang in there. It is worth it one hundred percent! *"Therefore I tell you, do not worry about your life, what you will eat or drink; or about your body, what you will wear. Is not life more important than food, and the body more important than clothes? Look at the birds of the air; they do not sow or reap or store away in barns, and yet your hea**venly Father feeds them.** Are you not much more valuable than they? Who of you by worrying can add a single hour to his life?*

And why do you worry about clothes? See how the lilies of the field grow. They do not labor or spin. Yet I tell you that not even Solomon-(he was a king)- in all his splendor was dressed like one of these. If that is how God clothes the grass of the field, which is here today and tomorrow is thrown into the fire, will he not much more clothe you, Oh you of little faith? So do not worry saying, 'What shall we eat?' or 'What shall we drink?' or 'What shall we wear?' For the pagans run after all these things, and your heavenly Father knows that you need them.

But seek first his kingdom and his righteousness, and all of these things will be given to you as well. Therefore do not worry about tomorrow, for tomorrow will worry about itself. Each day has enough trouble of its own.

Wow! Isn't that some wisdom given us by Jesus' teaching! He is forever reminding future generations not to worry! Did you know I once heard it said by a pastor of mine that worry can be considered a sin? It is not the act of worrying but digging a little deeper to its meaning. By worrying, we are all secretly doubting God in his plans for our individual lives. When we believe we do not or will not have what God says we will have in our lives, it is doubly hard to remain strong in our faith!

The Lord calls on us, ordinaries, to be bold in sharing the Gospel. We are not equipped to do that act of faith if we sit around continuously worrying and believing we can not do what he has called us to do. It will drive you crazy and you will worry until you make yourself nervous and then eventually a nervous wreck! Just kidding. But soon like me you will choose to believe there is no help for you and no way out of this trap that worry has caused. That is where my lesson learned comes in! I learned the very hard way to always, always let your worries go. Whether you write them down, (try going one step farther and eventually give them to God in prayer.) He hears you and knows the plans he has for your life! He knows every detail of his child's life. Because He has seen the days ahead and behind he was there and will be there with you. He will work all things out for the good of your wellbeing! Talk to someone you trust. An adult, a good family friend, your pets, anyone who will listen! Just please get it off your mind before it turns on you…. I eventually suffered a nervous breakdown from such behavior of keeping secret every single thing that worried me. This was in college and I was in my twenties before I received help, Please I am begging you, don't wait until worry brings on health issues! Do it now, get help! A little or a lot. Let someone know how you feel. Because, believe me, as well as they know you, they will never figure out what is going on inside. My family never saw it coming. I don't mean to alarm you, I am speaking from a dark place of mine. Which eventually I came crawling out of with professional help and their approach in medicine trials and techniques. I wish you only the best! And I hope I have offered some form of hope in these often dark areas of life and health.

Take care of yourselves and I hope everything turns out for the better in your life! I have truly enjoyed the journey as a writer, reader, and inspirational giver of hope! I pray that is what this adventure has been for you as well! Take care! And of course much love!

I don't want to leave you before presenting you with the opportunity to quiet your soul and consider accepting the unconditional love Jesus offers to all who invite him to live in their hearts. John 3:16 This act of faith will then allow you to love difficult people and go through trials with a smile when certain there is a greater, more perfect place waiting and a loving God to welcome you home. Heaven is, in fact, what God intended for the world to be at the beginning of time itself when He spoke life into the earth. With Jesus on your side, you will begin to see the permanent change in yourself that only He is capable. We can do nothing on our own. Only with God will we see a true shift in ourselves!...... I wish you only the best!

Sincerely,

Anna Hartsell

"I feel there's nothing truly more

artistic than loving people."

-Vincent

Printed in the United States
by Baker & Taylor Publisher Services